# Amelia Bedelia's
## •First Apple Pie•

Thanks, Grandma,
you're the apple of my eye too!

By Herman Parish
Pictures by Lynne Avril

Greenwillow Books
*An Imprint of HarperCollinsPublishers*

Hi Emma,
We had fun with you at the apple orchard. Have a great time this Fall. Lots of love, xxx
Abuelito and Abuelita ooo
10/15/2012

For Edna Frances
and Billy Rowe—H. P.

For Tim and Jane,
and to being grandparents!—L. A.

Herman would like to thank his wife, Rosemary, for contributing her apple pie recipe to this book.

Amelia Bedelia's First Apple Pie. Text copyright © 2010 by Herman S. Parish III. Illustrations copyright © 2010 by Lynne Avril.
Manufactured in China. For information address HarperCollins Children's Books,
a division of HarperCollins Publishers, 10 East 53rd Street, New York, NY 10022.
Gouache and black pencil were used to prepare the full-color art. The text type is Cantoria MT.
Amelia Bedelia is a registered trademark of Peppermint Partners, LLC.
Library of Congress Cataloging-in-Publication Data: Parish, Herman.
Amelia Bedelia's first apple pie / by Herman Parish ; illustrated by Lynne Avril. p. cm. "Greenwillow Books."
Summary: While visiting her grandparents, literal-minded Amelia Bedelia finally learns, despite some mishaps,
how to bake an apple pie. ISBN 978-0-06-196409-1 (trade bdg.) — ISBN 978-0-06-196410-7 (lib. bdg.)
ISBN 978-0-06-196411-4 (pbk.)
[1. Pies—Fiction. 2. Baking—Fiction. 3. Grandparents—Fiction. 4. Humorous stories.]
I. Avril, Lynne, (date) ill. II. Title. PZ7.P2185Arg 2010 [E]—dc22 2010009379
12 13 14 15 16 SCP 10 9 8 7 6 5 4 3 2 1

Greenwillow Books

**Amelia Bedelia** was visiting her grandparents. It was a glorious autumn afternoon—the perfect day to rake leaves into piles and run around the yard.

"Fall is in the air," said Granddad.

Granddad and Amelia Bedelia looked up.

"So are the birds," said Amelia Bedelia.

"V . . . W . . . What are they trying to spell?"

Just then Amelia Bedelia's grandma
came outside.
"Quick," said Granddad. "Look busy."
But it was too late.
"Hey, lazybones," Grandma said, jokingly.
"If you're just going to stand around,
I've got a job for you."

"What do you need?"
Granddad asked.
"Apples," said Grandma.
"I made pie dough. If you'll
get some apples, I can teach
Amelia Bedelia how to bake
an apple pie."

Grandma's apple pie was Amelia Bedelia's favorite.
"Hooray!" she yelled. "Race you to the car!"
She started to run but tripped over a branch
and landed right in the pile of leaves.

WHOOSH!

"How was your trip?" asked Granddad as he helped her up.
"Fun!" she said. "Fall is in the air and on the ground, too."
Granddad smiled and said, "Watch your step."

Amelia Bedelia tried to watch her steps, but it made
her dizzy to look down at her feet all the time.

Amelia Bedelia and Granddad were already in the car
when Grandma called out, "Be sure to pick up Granny Smith!"

"Who is Granny Smith? Is she helping us make the pie?"
Amelia Bedelia asked.
"You bet," Granddad said. "We couldn't do it without her."

Amelia Bedelia and Granddad drove out into the country.

"Your supermarket is far away," said Amelia Bedelia.

"We aren't going to the supermarket," said Granddad.

"We'll get our apples at the farmers' market."

"What?" asked Amelia Bedelia.

"Do we need to buy a farmer?"

"No," said Granddad, laughing.

"Their apples are much fresher."

"Apples are good for me, right?" asked Amelia Bedelia.

"Oh, yes," said Granddad. "An apple a day keeps the doctor away.
 They're good for your teeth, too. Folks call them nature's toothbrush."

"Hey, Granddad!" said Amelia Bedelia. "If I eat an apple a day,
 I won't have to go to the doctor or dentist ever again!"

Granddad smiled. "I wish it worked that way, pumpkin," he said.

Special!
GRANNY
SMITH

Granddad picked up a bright green apple, polished
it on his jacket, and tossed it to Amelia Bedelia.
"Nice catch," he said. "Meet Granny Smith."
Amelia Bedelia took a loud, crunchy bite.
"Granny is yummy," she said.

Winter
Banana

Black Twig

Greensleeves

Bushel baskets overflowed with red, yellow, orange, pink, and green apples. Some apples wore stripes or spots or splotches. The colors reminded Amelia Bedelia of autumn. While Granddad chose apples to buy, Amelia Bedelia read the names out loud. One kind was called "Delicious," but they all looked tasty to her.

Blaze

Royal Gala

Duchess

Golden Nugget

Northern Lights

Pink Pearl

Granny Smith

Delicious

When they got home, Grandma went
right to work coring and
peeling the apples.

Amelia Bedelia measured the peels to see which one was the longest.

Grandma
cut each apple into two pieces,

then into four pieces,

and then into
eight pieces.

Finally she sprinkled sugar and cinnamon on the slices.

Next Grandma pulled out all of her pie pans,
hunting for just the right one.
Amelia Bedelia found a tiny pan.
"Is this a toy?" she asked.

"No," said Grandma. "That is a real pie pan,
it's just really small. Aha! Here is the one I want.
Now please get me a little flour, sugarplum."

Amelia Bedelia spied a small flower
on the windowsill, and she picked it.
"Here you go, Grandma," she said.
"Thanks, sweetie," said Grandma.
Then she showed Amelia Bedelia
where she kept the flour she
used for baking.

Grandma rolled out the dough.
It got flatter and thinner.
It got rounder and bigger.
Grandma said, "Careful . . .
watch your fingers."

Amelia Bedelia took her hands off the table. She watched her fingers very carefully. They looked pretty boring. She wondered why she had to do this to make an apple pie.

"Now we need a sprinkle of flour," said Grandma. Amelia Bedelia reached into the sack of flour, grabbed a handful, and sprinkled it all over their heads. Grandma laughed. "Not on us," she said. "On the dough!" Amelia Bedelia sprinkled some on the dough, too.

"At last," said Grandma, "we're ready to put this pie together."
And that's exactly what Grandma and Amelia Bedelia did.
Then Grandma popped the pie into the oven, set the timer,
and started to clean up the kitchen.

That's when Amelia Bedelia had an idea.

She took the leftover
dough and rolled out
two small circles.

She put one in the little pie
pan, filled it with the extra apples,
and plopped the other circle on top.

Then she crimped
the edge all
around.

A smidgen of dough was left,
so she made a little flower—a tiny
daisy to decorate the top.

"Your mom and dad will be here soon," said Grandma.

"Then we'll have a pie party."

"Yippee!" said Amelia Bedelia.

Granddad heard the commotion and came into the kitchen.

"What are we celebrating?" he said.

"Honey," said Grandma, "Amelia Bedelia made her first apple pie."

After Grandma took her pie
out of the oven, Amelia Bedelia
carefully and secretly slid hers in.

"I am going to set this outside
to cool," said Grandma.

It was time to get ready for the party. Grandma hummed
as she set the table. Soon, Granddad was whistling the same tune.
Outside, the birds were chirping and tweeting and singing like mad.

"Listen!"
said Amelia Bedelia.

"It sounds like the birds
are having a party, too."

"My pie!"
exclaimed Grandma.

They all ran outside. The pie was covered with birds.
"Scram!" hollered Grandma. "Shoo, shoo!"

Chirp! Chirp! Chirp!

Amelia Bedelia took off her shoe
and handed it to Grandma, but
it was too late.
"Our pie!" said Amelia Bedelia.
"Gone!" said Grandma.

Just then, Amelia Bedelia's parents arrived.

Amelia Bedelia's dad stared at the empty pie pan.

"Gee," he said. "Couldn't you wait for us?"

"The birds ate our pie," said Amelia Bedelia.

"What birds?" asked her mom.

"I think they were swallows," said Granddad.

"They sure were," said Amelia Bedelia.

"They swallowed the whole thing."

"Well, sweetheart," said Amelia Bedelia's mother.
"Let's imagine how good it would have tasted
while we eat our ice cream."

The whole family tried to enjoy the ice cream
and not think about the pie, but that was impossible.

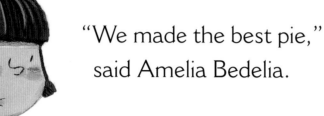

"We made the best pie,"
said Amelia Bedelia.

"It was a thing of beauty,"
said Grandma.

"It would have been
delicious," said Granddad.

"It was a perfect pie," said Amelia Bedelia.
Her lower lip trembled. She let out a sob.

"You know," said Amelia Bedelia's father. "Just hearing you talk about that pie makes me think I can smell a fresh-baked pie coming out of the oven."

"My pie!" exclaimed Amelia Bedelia.

They raced to the kitchen. Grandma took the tiny pie out of the oven and set it on the table. There it was: bubbling hot and baked to perfection. They all gathered around and gazed at it as though it were a brand-new baby.

"It's absolutely perfect,"
said Amelia Bedelia's mother.

"Just like Grandma's,"
said Granddad.

"Only smaller,"
said Amelia Bedelia.

"And you made it all by
yourself," said Grandma.

"This time," said Amelia Bedelia's father,
"let's let the pie cool down in the house."

But no one could wait. Grandma cut tiny pieces for everyone.
She took one bite and declared, "This is the best apple pie
I have ever tasted!"

Amelia Bedelia's smile was so big that it was hard for her to eat.

"Thank you, Grandma," she said. "And thank you, Granny."

"Granny who?" said Amelia Bedelia's mother.

"Granny Smith," said Amelia Bedelia. "She made all of our
apples in the first place."

# Amelia Bedelia's Apple Pie

## Important!
Make sure to have a parent or adult
help you in the kitchen!

## Crust

2 ½ cups flour
1 teaspoon salt
1 teaspoon sugar
¼ teaspoon cinnamon

2 sticks cold unsalted butter,
cut into small pieces
⅓ cup very cold water
1 tablespoon white vinegar

Combine the first four ingredients in a bowl. Add the butter and cut it into the flour thoroughly until the mixture resembles coarse crumbs, using two blunt dinner knives or a pastry blender.* Sprinkle the mixture with very cold water and vinegar. Mix this until the dough comes together and clears the side of the bowl. Gather the dough and shape into two flat, circular disks; wrap each disk separately in plastic wrap and refrigerate for at least one hour.

*This can also be done in a food processor: Pulse the flour mixture and butter until it resembles corn meal. Add the water and vinegar and pulse again until the dough comes together.

## Filling

8 cups peeled and thinly
sliced apples (any
variety except
Delicious)
½ cup flour
⅔ cup sugar

1 teaspoon cinnamon
¼ teaspoon nutmeg
2 tablespoons unsalted
butter, cut into small
pieces
½ lemon

Combine and mix the first five ingredients in a large bowl.

## Putting the pie together

Preheat the oven to 400 degrees.

Remove the dough from the refrigerator and allow it to rest at room temperature for about 5 minutes. Put the dough disks between two pieces of plastic wrap, and roll them out into two circles, each about 10 inches in diameter. Peel the plastic wrap off the top of the first circle of dough. Turn the dough, top side down, into a 9-inch pie pan, and peel the remaining plastic wrap off the dough in the pie pan. Add the apple mixture to the pie pan and dot the top with butter. Squeeze the juice of the lemon half over the mixture.

Peel one piece of plastic wrap off of the second dough circle and place it, top side down, over the apple mixture. Peel the remaining plastic wrap off of the pie dough. Pinch the top and bottom crusts together at the edge of the pan, and form a stand-up edge on the rim of the pie pan.

Cut 4–6 vent holes in the top of the crust (each vent should be about 1 inch long). Bake the pie in the center of the oven at 400 degrees for an hour, or until the pie is golden and the juices are thick and bubbly. Cool completely before serving.

(To make a young Amelia Bedelia-sized pie, cut all the ingredients in half, and use a 5-inch pie pan. Bake it for 40 minutes at 400 degrees.)